This book belongs to...

_____

_____

...who loves to read, and go on amazing adventures to imaginary worlds where animals can talk, pigs really can fly and magic makes the impossible possible!

COMING SOON

More fabulously funny, delightfully daft, and, tongue-twistingly-tastic stories!

TERRIBLE TEACHER

MISERABLE HEADMASTER

DINNER LADY DORIS

DISCO DAD

GRUMPY GRAMPS

MRS MOP

CELEBRITY CHEF

THE LAYABOUTS

REG'S VEG

Follow us on Twitter: @FayefairyB

Find us on Facebook: F.J. Beerling

Seriously Silly Stories

Greedy Grown Ups!

By

Beerling & Bryce

Introduction

Welcome to a world full of fantastically funny...

...super-silly

...laugh out loud stories with meaningful morals and alliteration throughout the pages of this brilliant book!

With slurpy-durps and double-dip, doubly delicious ice-creams on the menu; Super Slurp with his brand new, double-deluxe, double-door and double-decker ice-cream van was all set to put Stan out of business...

...But Stan had a plan - an old bicycle and a chunky fridge-freezer. Would Stan get on his bike and pedal his way to success? Or, would his dreams melt like ice-cream on a hot day?

Newsreader Norris was needy and greedy. He wanted fame and fortune and his face all over the news...

...He was the No.1 Newsreader and had a million-pound mansion and a massive ego to

match. But when he went from a crab catching champion to a cheating castle-crushing chump in just one day; would Norris mend his ways and part with his enormous ego or find himself down in the dumps - literally!

The annual, Cheesey Ched-Fest was a feast of festering flavours of epic cheese portions!

People came from far and wide to show off their wilting wonders! But their mouldy mounds melted in the hot sun, attracting mice - and chewing their way through the champion cheeses on display, the little furry fart balls now full of gas caused chaos and mass destruction..

The gone-off goat's cheese was giving people bad bellies too. The champion cheese chompathon had turned into a fart-fuelled festival of butt trumps and bad smells all round!

NEWSREADER NORRIS

NORRIS

...The Super-Star Show-off

Chapter 1–
Super-Sized Show-Off

In the small seaside town of Sandybottom, everyone was catching crabs**!**

It was the annual crusty crab catching competition!

A, flip-flopping, sand-slinging, nip-pinching, candyfloss chomping kind of event.

It took place on the beach, in the rocky rock pools and the piddly puddles created by the leaky Lido.

Children would pop their heads over the pier and wait with candyfloss baited breath for the crusty crabs to bite the bacon bits that were being used as bait.

The bunting was up, and buckets and spades were upside down as children patted them with spades and made super-duper sandcastles.

Parents paddled in the sea and grandparents dozed in their deckchairs. The smell of freshly cooked fish and chips wafted through the salty sea air. So too did the stinky stench of stomach-churning seaweed.

Off the beach and on top of Television Tower, its two-hundred foot tall aerial was whipping about in the wind. Inside Studio 7, newsreader Norris was preparing to cover this family day festival of fun.

A flip-flopping, beach ball bashing, crusty crab catching, sandy sandwich-filled fun at the beach!

As Norris sat in his dressing room, his teeth sparkled as they sizzled in solution. His Be-Bronze fake tan was going on and his wooden leg was coming off to be re-healed.

Norris stuck his toupee on with sticky tape and with a glint in his glass eye, he was now ready to read the news.

Meanwhile, on the beach, Norris's team of roving reporters were roasting in the hot sun. Norris had sent them packing with packed lunches, pocket-sized cameras and tiny tape recorders so they could cover the, crab-tastic event that Norris was going to take **all** the credit for!

Norris was not nice; Norris was greedy and selfish and his ego was enormous. He was a super-sized show-off who loved to see himself on the small screen. One day he hoped to see himself on the big screen too.

Off screen people loved him; he was popular with the public and was known as, 'Nice Norris the Number 1 newsreader.'

Back in Studio 7, nice Norris was not nice. He was even known as, not nice Norris the newsreader, and not nice Norris stole stories from his roving reporters and published them in newspapers.

Stealing stories and putting them into print
won Norris a lot awards - he even
received recognition for his roving
reporters hard work!

Back in Studio 7, Norris was now
newsreader ready. His team of personal
assistants had seen to his every need.
And Norris was very needy indeed.

As Norris stepped out of Television Tower's double doors and into his superstar, super-long stretched limo, his shoes were shined and his shoelaces were tied together...

...and stepping forward, Norris tripped falling face-first into a bucket of boiled bacon bait balls - **YUK!**

His chauffeur tried hard not to chuckle;
but his make-up team and camera crew
could not help but laugh their heads off.

Not nice Norris had a nasty niff about him
and was now covered in bait, but there was
no time to change, it was time for Norris to
cover the...

CRUSTY CRAB CATCHING COMPETITION!

Chapter 2
Something Fishy

The super-star, super-long, stretched limo was so long that it took twenty minutes for the driver to turn it around in the car park.

By the time he had turned it around, parked and opened the door to let Norris out. Norris demanded that he close the door and park on the beach - not beside the beach**!**

HOW DEMANDING WAS THAT!

"Why have you parked in a car park!" shouted Norris to his driver who was shaking in his boots.

"My public," added Norris, "are over there waiting for me." And with that, his driver got behind the wheel and spent another twenty minutes turning Norris's superstar, super-long, stretched limo back around and parked it on the beach not beside the beach.

"That's better," smiled Norris, as his adoring fans surrounded the superstar's, super-long, stretched limo and almost dragged him out of it as he went to get out...

...But no sooner had Norris stepped out to greet his fans; his fans could not get away from Norris quick enough!

The bacon bait balls had stuck to Norris's suit and started to stink. They had rotted in the heat and the seagulls could smell them as they circled Norris.

Circling turned to swooping as the hungry gulls began to bite on the bacon bait balls.

One seagull pecked at Norris's head before taking off with his toupee!

His fan's were stunned; Norris had no hair -
he was as bald as a baby's bottom!

The children taking part in the crab-catching
competition dropped their nets...

...The paddling parents stopped paddling and
looked on in horror as Norris pulled his
jacket up over his head to hide his balding
bonce.

As Norris dived for cover, he bashed his
balding bonce and almost knocked
himself out. Well, his fans fell about
laughing. His mum found it funny...

...and even the Town Crier was crying!

The roving reporters rolled about laughing. At last, a chance to get their own back on not nice Norris and his 'on air' diving disaster, or so they thought.

Norris meanwhile was digging about in the back of his superstar, super-long, stretched limo. He dug out a limp-looking floppy hat covered in flowers.

But Norris had no choice, he had to put it on his head to hide his balding bonce.

Attached to the hat was some fake
hair. Oh the shame! Poor Norris first
he had no hair, now he had plastic plaits
dangling from his floppy hat also
covered in felt flowers!

Norris put on his super-shady,
superstar sunglasses...

... and stepped out of his superstar,
super-long, stretched limo. "Oh look,"
said a little boy, "there's no-hair
Norris!" and with that Norris's fan fell
about laughing.

Norris ignored the laughter and stepped onto the sand. As he did so his wooden leg sank into the sand. Norris was ever so slightly 'wonky.'

As he started to talk, his fans leant to one side - the same side that Norris was slanting towards.

Norris got a sinking feeling; he wasn't wrong, Norris was sinking into the sand!

"Help"

he shouted hoping to be pulled out.

With the seagulls still swooping and biting his balding bonce, Norris was not in a good mood.

He was up to his neck in sand and now with crusty crabs nipping at his nose, Norris had had enough!

But help was at hand, or rather on the end of a fishing hook. One quick-thinking crabber cast out his line and caught Norris by his trouser belt.

He reeled Norris in, pulling him out of the sand before accidentally casting him out to the sea...

...A sea full of hungry sharks that started to circle poor Norris.

As Norris swam back towards the beach, a friendly fisherman caught Norris in his fishing net and scooped him up to safety, just in time!

Safely back on the shore, Norris pulled flapping fishes from his jacket pocket and put his floppy hat back on his balding bonce. He did look a sight - the cameras were still rolling...

...and Norris's fans were still rolling around with laughter.

"I'm sure to get the Golden Global Gong award for this," adding, "sensational seaside scoop of a story!" and with that Norris dried himself out in the sun, whilst posing for the cameras.

Norris was now being pecked at by a passing pelican. It was pecking at the fish that were flapping about in Norris's jacket pockets...

... his front pockets were full of fish; his wringing wet wig was full of winkles and crusty crabs were still clinging on to him - Norris was a walking rock-pool.

Crusty crabs clung to Norris's clothes;
he was covered in them. He picked
them off one by one, and as he did so, it
soon became clear that Norris had caught
the most crabs - Norris was declared the
winner...

... of the annual, Crusty Crab Catching
Competition.
Norris didn't even have a bucket of bait;
Norris **WAS** the bait**!**

Chapter 3
King of the Sandcastle

The roving reporters looked on in horror; there was no stopping Norris now.

Not only had he won the annual, Crusty Crab Catching Competition. His fans had tossed their toupees into the air to show their support for Norris.

It was a wig-flinging frenzy and a hair-raising experience all round.

The cameras were still rolling; Norris was back in the news - he was the news! He had made the headlines, his crab-catching chaos had been caught on camera.

Norris and his balding bonce were a seaside sensation. What started out as something fishy, was now the,

CATCH
OF
THE DAY!

The day was far from over; Norris still had to judge the sandcastle competition...

...meanwhile the roving reporters were raging - and set about scheming their revenge against Norris.

The children taking part in the competition stood proudly beside their tall turrets; their creative castles with double drawbridges and perfectly positioned pebbles placed all around them. They were a sandy sensation.

The Mayor marvelled at the magnificent
masterpieces and the Town Crier cried
with joy.

Norris stuck a flip flop onto the end of
his wooden stump to stop him sinking into
the sand and the photographer came and
took photographs of the creative
castles...

...that the children had cleverly crafted
from wet sand and salty sea water.

Making their way along a pebbly path that had been put into place; suddenly and without warning, a bacon bait ball bashed Norris on the back of his balding bonce.

Poor Norris, it knocked him to the ground and he landed flat on his face. As he lay sprawled out in the sun, he squashed several sandcastles. His feet flattened a few more, and even the Mayor stomped and stamped over what was left of the creative castles as he ran for cover.

The roving reporters revelled in their delight at the chaos caused by Norris. And, as the children stood crying, they watched their crumbling castles sink back into the sand.

The cameras continue to roll, capturing the events as they unfolded. Unfortunately for Norris, his popularity was plummeting fast. People who had tuned in to watch him, now turned their T.V's off!

Norris had to think fast, he had to do something to restore his ratings and save his reputation.

Grabbing a small bucket and spade, Norris started to sculpt more sandcastles. But Norris was no artist, and, despite his best efforts, his tall turrets toppled, flopped and fell over. His sandcastles crumbled.

And, to make matters worse, it had started to rain. Norris had gone from being a crusty crab catching champion to a castle-crushing chump all in one day!

And just like the weather, Norris's career was a complete washout.

The children were still crying, the Mayor was miserable and even the cameraman was cross because he had to stop filming.

But needy, greedy Norris had to stay in the news -he **WAS** the news!

His enormous ego and million-pound mansion needed paying for -and without a pay packet Norris had no other income, he could be kicked out.

Chapter 4
Shark's Tale

Eventually, it stopped raining; the clouds cleared and the sun came out, so did 'Super-Slurp' the ice-cream van.

It tootled and tinkled as it shot across the sand and parked up by some swings. The cameras were rolling as Norris looked on in horror at the hoards of children lining up to cool themselves down. Super-Slurp was serving up an impressive selection of ice-lollies...

...From chocci-wocci chewy chocolate chip, to cheeky cherry, sizzling strawberry and even fizzle-licious lemonade licks!

It was a, **SUPER-SLURP** sensation.

Mr Slurp was making a mint! And selling mint chocci-chip choc ices too. Norris was not amused! He was fuming, he was not being filmed, it was not his face in front of the camera capturing the crowds.

Norris put his hands into his pocket and pulled out a wet wallet, covered in crusty crabs clinging on to it.

One by one, Norris picked off the crusty crabs and flipped-flopped back across the soggy sand towards Mr Slurp in his impressive ice-cream van.

He pushed his way to the front of the queue, looked up at Mr Slurp and said, "Did you know you've got a flat tyre?" Mr Slurp frowned and went to take a look. No sooner had he stepped out of the ice-cream van, Norris quickly nipped inside and locked the door.

"**HEY**," shouted Mr Slurp, banging his fist on the door. "Get out," he added. But Norris was not listening. He was busy feeding the kids freebies and given them all brain-freeze.

The whirly-whips were given away first. Followed by the fudge-tastic, super-slushy slurps...

...The dreamy-creamy, caramel-coated, crunchy-coconut choc-ices.

It was a free for all, a face-filling, ice-cream carnival of crunching and munching.

Eventually there was nothing left to give away, so Norris threw away the empty boxes and flung chocolate flakes out through the serving hatch.

As the children caught them, Norris squirted them with strawberry sauce and covered them in sprinkles that melted in the hot sun.

The children looked more like crispy choc ices than kids! They were a chewy-gooey, sticky, sweet-smelling mess and had caught the attention of the greedy seagulls.

The seagulls flapped their wings and flew towards the children as they stood stuffing their faces...

...it was a feather-flapping frenzy. The greedy gulls dive-bombed the unsuspecting children, pecking at their heads as panicked parents flapped their arms about hoping to scare them off.

Whilst all this was going on, the ice-cream van was going up in smoke!

It had over heated and Norris did not know what to do. "Turn the fan on," shouted Mr Slurp from outside the ice-cream van. "How do I do that?" Quizzed Norris from inside the ice-cream van.

"Turn the key," added Mr Slurp who was now panicking and trying to climb into the ice-cream van through the small serving hatch!

SOLD OUT

Norris turned the wrong key! Instead of switching the fan on, the engine came on and it was already in gear...

...reverse gear! The ice-cream van shot backwards across the sand. Mr Slurp was still stuck in the small serving hatch. His legs were dangling and donking people on the back of their heads, knocking them down like dominoes. It got worse when his legs swiped the deckchairs, folding them in half, trapping the grandparents inside!

The roving reporters could not believe their luck. The continuing chaos caused by Norris had been caught on camera - again!

And it continued when the zig-zagging ice-cream van, with a nervous Norris inside, and a scared-stiff Mr Slurp hanging onto the small serving hatch, shot straight into the shark-infested sea.

The hungry sharks circled the slow-sinking ice-cream van.

Instead of trying to climb into the serving hatch, Mr Slurp was now trying to back out of it and climb onto the top of the ice-cream van!

Norris had the same idea, and, between them they managed to clamber onto its roof and cling onto the giant pink plastic ice-cream cone.

The cameraman was laughing so much that he could not keep his camera straight.

Whilst the ice-cream van was filling up with water; the ice-cream making machine was emptying itself out into the sea - spilling a sludge of sticky smooth

strawberry ice-cream. The hungry sharks sucked it all up! It gave them a sugar-rush and sent them spinning around in circles until the sugar wore off.

Norris needed to distract the sharks, but had nothing left to throw at them except for Mr Slurp but he wasn't going to do that!

The sharks had sucked up all the strawberry sludge and were now snapping at Mr Slurp's legs!

The ice-cream van's tinkle had tonked. It now sounded more like whale music than

tinkling tunes. This attracted even more sharks and as Mr Slurp looked down, it looked more like shark soup than the deep blue sea!

Still clinging onto the giant pink plastic ice-cream cone; they started to lose their grip, but just as they could not cling on any longer, help was at hand, or rather on the end of a rope ladder.

Hovering high above their heads was the, News Now helicopter. It had been filming the fiasco and was now filming their rescue!

Not the news headlines Norris had been hoping for; but for the millions tuned in to watch, it was worth watching - it was a complete disaster - and for Norris...

...he finally got his wish, to appear on the big screen - but not drenched and

half drowned, clinging onto a giant pink plastic ice-cream cone with hungry sharks snapping at his legs, whilst sinking five-miles out to sea with Mr Slurp the ice-cream man!

Norris's hopes of being nominated as the

NUMBER ONE NEWSREADER

had just been swept out to sea. It was a, corn popping, a cookie-crunching, tea-time television triumph for the viewers and revenge for the roving reporters, who roared with delight at Norris's demise.

But all was not lost; Norris and Mr Slurp,
who were still clinging onto the giant pink
plastic ice-cream cone, looked up as the
rope ladder dangled down.

And just in time too. As they clung onto
the rope ladder and were lifted up - the
ice-cream van was swallowed up by the sea.
It sunk to the sounds of gurgling and
slurping and swirling, sucked into the sea
and never to be seen again.

Chapter 5
From Greedy to Needy

As the News Now helicopter flew back
to shore and landed safely on the beach;
the crowds clapped and cheered. They
were full of praise for... Mr Slurp**?!**

They thought that Mr Slurp had saved
Norris from the shark infested sea.
Norris was not amused, nobody had saved
him. But the crowds greeted Mr Slurp as
a hero. They paraded him around the
promenade as Norris slumped down in the
sand and watched as Mr Slurp was
awarded the 'Have a go Hero' Medal for
bravery, but that was not all...

...Mr Slurp was also given a brand new,
top of the range, super-duper, deluxe
ice-cream van.

Its tinkle played ten different tunes. Its super-speedy ice-cream making machine made five different flavours of ice-cream...

...all at once. And instead of a giant pink plastic ice-cream cone on top it was fitted with a second serving deck!

Hot dogs, beefy burgers and crunchy candyfloss - Mr Slurp was back in business.

Meanwhile, Norris was out of business. He had been sacked for sloppy workmanship - all day long he had caused chaos; made kids cry by crushing their sandcastles and cheated in the crusty crab catching competition by using himself as bait.

All because Norris was not nice; Norris was greedy. He wanted to be famous, fabulous, loved, liked, admired and adored. Instead, he had turned into a super-star show off and people had gone off him. They even switched their television sets off when Norris came on.

Needy, greedy Norris lost his million-pound mansion and was now living in a wheely bin by the beach.

He had cold bacon bait balls for breakfast and cold chips for dinner washed down with a slurpy-durp courtesy of Mr Slurp, every time he drove past.

At the end of the day when the beach cleaners had cleared off, Norris helped himself to leftovers left in the beach bins.

From half eaten hamburgers to chomping

on cold, hard chips and even fried fish heads. He would wash in the sea and dry out in the sun. Norris who was once the Number 1 Newsreader was now a nobody with no job.

Despite all this, Norris still had an enormous ego and loved the sound of his own voice. So when the perfect position became available, Norris was just the man for the job.

Every time he wanted to hear the sound of his own voice, all he had to to was talk to Tom - the talking clock and hear himself speak.

Norris was good at his job and very soon he was able to upgrade from a wheely bin beside the beach - to a beach hut on the beach.

When Norris had saved some more money, he was able to buy a new, second-hand suit and got a new job as a bingo ball caller. At first only a few people came along, they still did not like Norris, but they did like bingo.

After a while, they warmed to Norris and he parted ways with his enormous ego. He would dress up as a pirate, with a real wooden leg, a wonky wig and even a glass eye - Norris was the perfect pirate and now the people loved him.

The people praised him, they applauded him and they even threw their pennies at him. After all, every little helped!

Norris popped his pennies into a pot and very soon he was able to pay for his own pad. It was modest, unlike his million-pound mansion; it was small but not as small or smelly like the wheely bin was, but, more importantly it was home and it had a real front door and not a battered old bin lid!

STAN THE ICE-CREAM MAN

...EVERYONE'S FAVOURITE!

Chapter 1
Taste-Tingling Triumph

Stan was an ice-cream man; he was everyone's favourite ice-cream man.

His fantastic fruit flavoured chewy, chompy, choc-ices and fizzle-licious ice lollies were perfect for cooling everyone

down on a hot day. As Stan drove around, he operated a 'Park up and Pay' system. He would park up and people would pay. His musical melodies could be heard from miles around and people came from miles around to crunch and munch on his caramel-coated choc-ices and whirly whips ice-creams.

Stan was so popular he was even granted permission to park his ice-cream van outside the gates of Buckingham Palace...

...The tourists did get a treat.

Yes, Stan was everyone's favourite. He loved selling ice-creams so much that he even had *TWO* ice-cream vans! Yes two, a perfectly pink one and a, brilliant blue one.

Even a flat type could not stop Stan from selling his fabulous, fruity flavoured slurpy-durps and doubly delicious chewy, caramel flavoured double choc choc-ices.

Every year, Stan would travel by train to the, Ice-cream Cone convention - a flaky-flurry, a festival of fantastic new flavours. A crispy-coated carnival of crunchiness and a coin-swapping extravaganza!

Ice-cream sellers from across the country came and took part in this taste-tingling triumph. A taste and take-home triumph. They would scoop their silver spoons into pots of peanut munch and buttercream crunch. Sample sugary flavoured ices like wonder mint whirls

and spearmint twirls that tingled on their tongue. Funky fudge flakes and little coffee trumpet truffles were the fizzle-licious flavours of the day and, the sugary sherbet shoes had a real kick to them!

The cherry blossom bombs went off with a bang and the Tutti-fruitti flavoured frosty flakes tasted fabulous. And when the marzipan Peter Pans were popped into people's mouths, everyone felt like a big kid - even the delightful dribbly-drools did their job and made everyone's mouth water.

Little fizzy fountains of flavoured water were dotted about for people to pop their plastic beakers into and enjoy a refreshing drink.

The huge hall was full of stalls and
stands and pretty pop-up tents,
tempting people to step inside and
sample their wafting waffle-wonders;
their treacle-toffee treats and their
dreamy-creamy ice-cream cones.

Stan did not know what to stuff his
face full of first. Every stand had a
sugary-sweet sensation to sell and every
flavour to savour. Stan made his way
along all the stalls and from stand to
stand filling his bags full of fruity-
flavoured freebies.

He filled his mouth full with mouth-watering marshmallows and rhubarb and raisin flavoured flakes.

He dipped his fingers into chocolate-flavoured figs. He chomped on chewy chocolate-covered currants and sucked up sherbet syrup through a straw. Stan was on a sugar-fuelled frenzy; his belly was so fat that his buttons started to pop!

Stan waddled along the rest of the stalls; looking, listening and liking what he could see and smell.

Amazing melodies tinkled and tootled playing tinkling tunes. From tiny trumpets

to tremendous trombones and even brass bands belting out belters. There was a musical melody for everybody. Still stuffing his face with chewy-gooey, penguin pillow marshmallows and popular polar bear pear-drops. Stan made his way towards the ice-cream van stand, It was an amazing sight to see.

Stan's eyes were on stalks as he spied top of the range ice-cream vans...

...double deluxe with double-door serving hatches...

...and super-sized sprinkle shakers; super-long, super-speedy and super expensive too!

Some had massive menus and cup-cake sized ice-cream cones, and robotic arms to curl and twirl super-soft, dreamy-creamy ice-creams in super-quick time.

Stan could only dream of owning one of these, dreamy, double-deluxe, double-door ice-cream vans. But with his fabulous new flavours, and a bag full of freebies, Stan had enough to entice his customers to part with their pennies.

That was until Stan spied Mr Super Slurp himself buying a brand new, double-deluxe, double-door, double-decker ice cream van, and that it where our story begins...

Stan dropped his bags, spilling freebies all over the floor. He almost cried when he saw Mr Slurp shaking hands with Susan the sales lady. This could only mean one thing...

...Mr Slurp was just about to super-size his profits with a brand new, double-deluxe, double-door and double-decker ice cream van.

Not only that, but it came stocked with super-soft sorbets, fitted with chest-sized chillers, hot-dog holders and beefy burger baskets. It was a burger-burping fest of fabulous flavours in one van.

It was a dream machine and Mr Slurp was the proud owner of not one but three of these, double-deluxe, double-door and double-decker ice-cream, money-making machine on wheels.

Whirly-whips, sparkly sprinkles, super-soft whippy-wonders to chewy choc-ices and now perfect pizzas and beefy burgers were also on the menu.

But not on Stan's menu. Stan had to make do with his single-shut serving hatch, single-decker and single-seat vintage ice cream machine. It didn't have robotic arms, Stan had to spread the sprinkles himself.

Poor Stan, he picked his freebies up
from off the floor and popped them back
into his bag.

He looked up and looked across the hall;
he could not help feeling deflated, just
like the tyres on his spare ice-cream van.
Just then Mr Slurp sped past him in his
double-deluxe, double-door and double-
decker ice-cream van.

As if things weren't bad enough for Stan;
Mr Slurp had also just hired the fastest
flake-flingers in the country. Not only
could they chuck chunky chocolate flakes
into ice-cream cones in double-quick time,
they could also fling fondant-flavoured

ice-creams into cones in an instant!
But, all was not lost, Stan still had a few
stalls left to visit. He dragged his bags
behind him, when suddenly something
caught his eye and sent his taste bugs
tingling...

His nostrils twitched and he dribbled and drooled with delight at the most magnificent sight that Stan had ever seen.

It was a marvel, it was magnificent, it was a, multi-function, money-making machine of epic proportions. It was magical, and it was going home with Stan, whether he could afford it or not. It was a super-scoop, a seven-flavoured serving ice-cream making machine and before he knew it, Stan had sold his house for one!

Stan was now the owner of the only one of its kind anywhere in the world and was going back home with him...

...in a wheelbarrow. It was far too big to carry or drag around. Stan had to ask for help to lift it up and onto the goods wagon at the train station.

The station master and porter helped Stan load it onto the good wagon. Stan sat on the floor with his arms around his new money-making ice-cream making machine.

Chapter 2
The Tinkle That Tonked

A few days later, Stan was back in business and back in the driving seat of his beloved, single-door, single-decker and single-seater vintage ice-cream van.

He tinkled and tootled as he drove around town and whistled as he went.

Stan noticed how quiet it was; there were no children - anywhere!

The parks were empty...

...and at Stan's, park up and pay places there were spaces where there where usually queues of kids, waiting for Stan's fabulous, frosty, fruity-flavoured lollies.

"What's going on?" said Stan to himself. "Where are all the children, why is the town so quiet all of a sudden?" Stan didn't have to wait long for an answer. As he continued to tootle and tinkle, Mr Slurp sped past in his double-door, double-deluxe and double-decker ice-cream van. It was going so fast it sent Stan's pink plastic ice-cream cone spinning up into the air before crashing back down onto the ground.

Stan's tinkle had tonked; his marvellous musical melodies had been silenced and Stan stood in silence as he watched Mr Slurp spin around the corners and disappear from view. He had stolen Stan's park up and pay pitches right from under his nose.
Stan was fuming!

Stan had no customers and a freezer full of famous, fruity-flavoured ice-lollies and ice-creams, but no ordinary ice-creams; Stan had installed his magnificent, super seven-scoop, money-making ice-cream machine, and needed to sell some ice-creams.

Stan came up with a plan; all he had to do to win his customers back was to get up earlier than Mr Slurp in his double-door, double-deluxe and double-decker ice-cream making machine.

It sounded simple enough, and sure enough the next morning; half way through the night, Stan got up, got dressed and got going.

He whizzed around town, tinkling and tootling as he went. Turning up the tunes, so everybody heard him - and they did, they all woke up! It wasn't a dawn chorus, it was a sunrise surprise. The surprise was that Stan was up before the sun, this did not go down too well with people still in their beds!

The Mayor was not amused; the Town Crier cried and the parents protested when their children chorused, "we want ice-cream" at four in the morning!

Mr Slurp who had fallen asleep in his chair the night before was rudely awoken by

the children's chants.

He opened his front door and stepped out into the street. He soon smiled when he saw Stan being given his marching orders from the Mayor and chuckled when the Town Crier turned his back on Stan, giving him the cold shoulder. Stan did not see Mr Slurp standing out in the street rubbing his hands together.

Chapter 3
Cold As Ice

Poor Stan had been left out in the cold - he had locked himself out when he went out and now he could not get back in.

So, he went around the back and in through the side gate.

It was breakfast time so Stan decided to make himself some breakfast. "Burnt bacon here we come," he said rubbing his hands together.

All that early morning tootling and tinkling around town had made Stan very hungry.

First, he fried some eggs, but that didn't
go too well...

So he set to work on burning some bacon.
First he filled a frying pan with some fat,
a lot of fat. Then he went outside to
check that the ice-cream van was
charging. But it wasn't plugged in and when
Stan opened the van door, a slurry of
slushy ice-cream whooshed passed him and
sent Stan sliding down the driveway.

The sticky sludge soon set hard in the hot
sun, cementing Stan to the spot, Stan was
stuck fast!

Stan was not having a very good day, and it was about to get a whole lot worse, when suddenly...

...the bacon had burnt a hole in the frying pan and the fat set light to the gas cooker which then exploded and blew up the house!

Soon, some smouldering cinders, a few bricks and a very burnt frying pan were all that was left of Stan's house.

Poor Stan was still stuck to the spot. Luckily for him, the heat from the fire melted the slushy sludge and set Stan free. He was able to fling his arms about and cry for help. But it was too late, his house had burnt to the ground. There was nothing left apart

from his perfectly pink and brilliantly blue
ice-cream vans...

...and, to make matters worse, who should
turn up and turn on his tinkling tunes?
Yep, none other than Mr Slurp himself
with a super-sized grin across his face.
Not only had he pinched Stan's park up
and pay pitches along with all his
customers, but Mr Slurp was now the only
mobile ice-cream man with an ice-cream
van for miles around.

Stan's dreams of becoming the best ice-cream man ever had just melted right in front of him.

He stepped out of his sticky sludge and walked over to what was left of his house. He was about to burst into tears when suddenly he spotted something sparkling amongst the smouldering ashes.

Stan could not believe his luck. His fridge-freezer and his Grandad's old bike had also survived the fire!

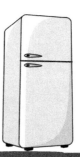

Stan's first challenge was to move his fridge-freezer. So, grabbing a pair of roller skates, Stan fixed the wheels onto the bottom of the fridge-freezer, gave it a little push and off it went...

..."ha," said Stan, "that was easy," and with that he secured the fridge-freezer onto the front of his Grandad's old bike; which wasn't very easy.

Stan did not realise just how heavy the fridge-freezer was. When he sat down in the seat on his bike and began to peddle; Stan was going nowhere fast.

He puffed and pedalled and pedalled and puffed but it was no use. The fridge-freezer was too heavy for Stan to push - Stan needed a new idea...

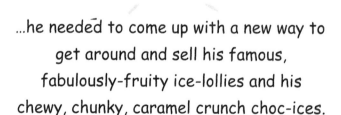

...he needed to come up with a new way to get around and sell his famous, fabulously-fruity ice-lollies and his chewy, chunky, caramel crunch choc-ices.

Just then, Stan's next door neighbour who had been watching Stan, gave him some advise. "If you push that bike to the top of the hill and get on, you won't have to peddle, it will roll down the hill all by itself." "What a good idea," thought Stan and with that he did just that - he puffed and he pushed; he pushed and he puffed all the way to the top of the hill. People stopped to take pictures of Stan

pushing an old bike with a fridge-freezer strapped onto it, up to the top of the hill; what a funny thing to see.

Stan didn't test the brakes before he got on his bike and shot off down the hill at super-sonic speed with a fridge-freezer strapped onto the front.

He held on to the handle bars for deal life and was going so fast that he shot past Mr Slurp in his double-deluxe, double-door and double-decker ice-cream van.

Stan was going to fast that he broke the sound barrier. He was shouting, "ices, ices, get your choc ices," as he shot past people and managed to take their money before flinging ice-creams at their faces and the flake-flinging fiasco almost ended in disaster as Stan's wheels wobbled all over the place.

Stan tinkled his bike bell as he shot past people, they were laughing their heads off. Stan's little bike bell did not sound the same as his marvellous musical melodies...

...it didn't even tinkle, it tinked!

Stan's drive-by, flake-flinging, had left him covered in caramel and coated in chocolate. He looked more like an ice-cream than an ice-cream man.

Everybody that Stan shot past that day were still laughing their heads off that night. The sight of Stan's wheels wobbling and his fridge-freezer lid flapping as he sped off at super-sonic speed was the funniest thing that they had ever seen.

The Mayor was so amazed by Stan that he awarded him a medal for being funny. Stan was officially the village idiot. But Stan did not care, Stan was back in business and the Mayor was also so impressed by Stan's determination to make money, he was given the keys to a brand new, double-deluxe, double-door and double-decker ice-cream van. With twenty different twinkling tunes, and a young apprentice to help, Stan could serve up a treat when it got busy.

Stan really was back in business -
serving up slurpy-durps and seven
sensational flavoured ice-creams all at
once from his marvellous, amazing ice-
cream making machine. He sold more
ice-creams than Mr Slurp and even
managed to get his park up and pay
pitches back. It was a whippy-dippy,
flake-fest of chewy, chocci caramel
coated crunchiness of choc-ices and
frutti-tutti tongue-twistingly-tastic
ice-lollies all round!

105

THE CHEESY CHED-FEST!

Chapter 1
The Annual Ched-Fest

In the little village of Chedderton, it was the annual, Cheesy Ched-Fest Event. A creamy, cracker-crunching , cheese chomping, stinky, stringy cheesy kind of event.

A festival of festering flavours. Everyone was crackers and they would travel from Wensleydale and Wilton to take part in this cheesy-chomping competition.

They rolled up in their cars and rolled their massive mounds down the hill and into the triangular tents that had been tied down with cheese strings!

They spread their whiffy wonders out across the tables to tempt the cheese tasters.

Their festering flavours ranged from Stinky Socks to the Bishop's Boot. Even cheese from overseas were entered into the competition of wilting wonders that were on display. Pegs and programmes were available from the first-aid tent!

Cheese sandwiches, cheese rolls, cheese burgers, cheese strings and even cheesecakes were available to buy from the...cheese counter!

As well as the cheese-fest of festering flavours, there was also a ched-off, a chewy cheese chomping competition. A, chuck the cheddar, bash a brie, and even a whiff and sniff quiz.

The annual Ched-Fest always took part on the hottest day of the year and this year, things were really hotting up - so too were the cheeses as they started to bubble and boil. It was smellier than ever and now with new cheeses taking part...

...from 'awful armpit' to 'flaky foot fungus' and even, 'cheesy feet' flavours! It was a smouldering stink-fest of epic cheese portions.

111

It was a triumph; an aromatic aroma of awfulness. A, peg-popping pong-a-thon and an, 'all you can eat,' chewy, cheese chompathon.

It could be seen and smelt for miles around, and this attracted mice - a lot of mice. The mice would meet up in their millions and march across the meadows with dreams of munching on the mouldy mounds of champion, churned cheeses.

It was a furry four-feet free food fest!

The mice dodged the mouse marshals and the mouse traps by burrowing deep under the ground and pop up inside the pop-up tents above ground.

They climbed up the table legs and chomped and chewed their way through chunks of champion cheeses. Hollowing out holes as they went in through one side, and came out the other side.

Their furry little bellies were full of cheese and...flatulence! (wind). Their farts were so powerful that each time they popped, it propelled them up into the air!

This year was no different; as the people turned up, so too did the mice and the big cheese himself - the Mayor of Chedderton, Mr Grate. He officially declared the annual Ched Fest open after cutting the cheese-string ribbon.

The brass band was playing in the background, the wind wafted through the air and sent the mice into a mouth-watering munch-up.

The ched-fest was well under way when Mr and Mrs Moore turned up, parked up and took part. Their massive monster truck had a trailer attached to it. In the trailer was their massive, monster-sized mound of mouldy cheese. Festering away in the hot sun it was a stinkfest all of its own...

...its mould had mould! And from miles around, mini mouse-sized mouths were watering at the sight of it. And even before Mr Moore had the chance to unload it; ten million tiny teeth had chewed and chomped their way through it.

By the time Mr Moore had managed to shoo the mice away; their mouldy, monster-sized mound was no bigger than a cheese ball! Mr Moore was furious; he ripped up his registration papers...

...and watched as the tiny terrors took away his only chance of winning the Ched-fest champion cheese trophy. Not only that, the mice had also gorged on his gone-off goats cheese which he was saving as part of his plans to sabotage the Cheesy Ched-fest.

Mr and Mrs Moore lived up to their name - they always wanted more. More of everything and by giving out gone off goats cheese, they gave everyone bad bellies! This meant that Mr and Mrs Moore could help themselves to the cheeses that were on display and in a greedy, grab and go, they also helped themselves to the tins of creamed cheeses too!

How deliciously devious was that!

Chapter 2
Grated Expectations

Unable to put his plan into action; Mr
Moore put on his over-sized overcoat
instead; it was full of over-sized pockets.
He made his way over to the cheese-
chomping tent and joined in with the
Ched-fest.

Cheese-chomping tent

As Mr Moore chomped and chewed his way through the cheap-tasting cheeses; he picked up a packet of cheese and popped it into one of his many pockets. And, making his way along the many tables, even more packets of cheeses were popped into his many pockets.

It was a, pocket-popping, packet packing, fill...

By the time he had finished chomping; his pockets were packed full of packet cheeses and cheese-chomping mice! A cheese-chomping mouse.

His over-sized overcoat was heavy and he was hot as he made his way into and out of the cheese-tasting tents.

Wondering why the cheap-tasting cheeses tasted so 'cheap,' Mr Moore's belly began to bubble and he began to burp and he wasn't the only one.

All around him were bulging bellies and burping!

Their bulging bellies bubbled and their bottoms exploded - it had turned into a cheese-chomping, stomach-churning, butt-trumping, festival of foul-flavours and mouldy misgivings of epic proportions and, it was about to get a whole lot worse!

Mini Mouse Circus

In the next field; Magnificent Mike and his mini mouse circus had pulled up. Their tent was pitched up and the mice were warming up when suddenly their little noses started to twitch and tingle with delight when the aroma of whiffy wilts wafted through the air and seeped in to the big top tent. The putrid pong of bad belly butt trumps mixed with mouldy cheese was too tempting - the trapeze mice flew through the air and out of the little hole in the top of the big top. The wire-walking mice walked out, and the mice that were clowning around in little toy cars; tinkled and tootled and trundled into the next field and into the Cheesy Ched-Fest.

They took took part in the chomping and chewed their way through the massive mounds of mouldy cheeses, until only a few crumbs were left. They even chewed through the cheese strings that were used to tie the tents down with!

It was now a cheese-less, fowl-smelling stink-fest of festering farts filling the air.

It wasn't just the mice that were popping-people were popping all over the place. The air was full of a smelly smouldering-smog; the flowers flopped, the wheat wilted and the grass gave up!

The roses rotted and the buttercups got a bashing; even the weeping willows wept.

The green haze from the putrid pong hung in the air but people didn't hang around, the made their way back to their cars, butt-trumping and burping as they went.

They could not get away quick enough. They could not escape the smell that was escaping from their bottoms and they could not escape the ten-thousand tiny teeth that had chomped and chewed their way through the cheeses- and they went home with them!

They hid in hats; burrowed in handbags and clung onto coats as what was left of the cheeses were packed away and bunged into car boots along with the little furry fart-balls, they also had bad bellies from eating the gone-off goats cheeses.

The car park was in chaos as people panicked to get their cars into gear and get out of there as quickly as possible. The Cheesy Ched-Fest had turned into a farce and the farmer who had hired out his meadow was now left with holes the size of houses from the cheese-chomping mice!

On the way back home, all people could hear were pinging and popping sounds coming from the boot of their cars.

The little furry fart-balls were pinging all over the place as they popped. It was a ping-pong, fart-athon, turning the air green with gone-off gut gas.

Well, that's what you get for being greedy. Chomping and chewing on champion cheeses whilst trying to cheat your way into winning the 'Wilting Wonders' winners cup!

Giving out gone-off goat's cheeses, and getting greedy by always wanting more. Mr and Mrs Moore certainly got more than they bargained for. They had at least two thousand, furry little fart-balls popping and pinging about in the boot of their car and in need of a new home.

And the moral of this story is, if you're needy and greedy, you will always get more than you bargained for.

128